THE DUCK WHO DIDN'T LIKE WATER

STEVE SMALL

A Paula Wiseman Book
Simon & Schuster Books for Young Readers
New York   London   Toronto   Sydney   New Delhi

For Monica

SIMON & SCHUSTER BOOKS FOR YOUNG READERS

An imprint of Simon & Schuster Children's Publishing Division

1230 Avenue of the Americas, New York, New York 10020

© 2021 by Steve Small

Jacket design by Tom Daly © 2021 by Simon & Schuster, Inc.

First published in Great Britain in 2021 by Simon & Schuster UK Ltd.

First US edition March 2021

All rights reserved, including the right of reproduction in whole or in part in any form.

SIMON & SCHUSTER BOOKS FOR YOUNG READERS

and related marks are trademarks of Simon & Schuster, Inc.

For information about special discounts for bulk purchases, please contact Simon & Schuster

Special Sales at 1-866-506-1949 or business@simonandschuster.com.

The Simon & Schuster Speakers Bureau can bring authors to your live event.

For more information or to book an event, contact the Simon & Schuster Speakers Bureau

at 1-866-248-3049 or visit our website at www.simonspeakers.com.

The text for this book was set in Museo Slab.

Manufactured in China

1220 SUK

2 4 6 8 10 9 7 5 3 1

Library of Congress Control Number: 2020947281

ISBN 9781534489172

ISBN 9781534489189 (ebook)

There was once a duck
who didn't like water.

Duck didn't like swimming in it . . .

or paddling in it.

PLOP!

And Duck didn't like it
when it rained.

PLIP!

Not even if it rained just a little bit.

PLOP!

On rainy days, Duck liked nothing more than curling up with a good book and a hot drink.

I don't need to go outside,
Duck thought. *I've got
everything I need right here.*

And mostly that was true.

SIGH

One very windy and rainy night,
Duck was woken up by a loud noise . . .

and discovered a hole in the roof.

Well, I can't fix that tonight, Duck thought.

So Duck popped outside for a bucket . . .

and found an unexpected visitor,
who was lost. Very lost.

"Why don't you rest here for the night
where it's warm and dry?" asked Duck.

Frog cheerfully agreed, even though Frog
liked water *very* much.

The next morning, Duck said,
"We need to get you home,
but first we need to find out
where home actually is."

"Okay," said Frog.

RIBBIT

So off they went.

They searched
EVERYWHERE . . .

but they couldn't find
Frog's home,

so they stopped for some lunch.

They set off again, but no
matter who they asked,

or where they looked,

they STILL couldn't find Frog's home.

So that night they ate dinner,
read each other stories,

said good night,

G'NIGHT

and went to bed.

RIBBIT

The next morning, Pelican dropped by.
"Hello, Frog. You're a long way from home."

"Wait!" said Duck. "Do you know where Frog lives?"

"Sure! It's all the way over in the next river," Pelican replied. "Need a lift?"

By way of a goodbye, Duck gave Frog
two gifts: a good book and
a small umbrella.

Frog said a BIG
thank-you.

RIBBIT

And moments later, Frog was gone.

Days went by. Everything was
the same as before.

But it felt different.

Something
was missing.

PLIK!

PLIK!

So Duck
set off.

And though it rained and it poured . . .

and the wind blew this way . . .

and that,

Duck did not give up.

Until, quite suddenly . . .

Duck found Frog!

"Home doesn't feel like home
if you're not there!" Duck said.

And Frog agreed.

So Duck and Frog returned to their
old routines. They visited their new friends,

read stories to each other, and,

perhaps most importantly of all . . .

they fixed the hole in the roof.